8
Hal - le - lu - jah, Hal - le - lu - jah, Hal-le - lu-
Hal - le - lu - jah, Hal - le - lu - jah, Hal-le - lu - jah,
Hal - le - lu - jah, Hal - le - lu - jah, Hal-le - lu - jah, Hal-le - lu - jah, Hal-
Hal - le - lu - jah, Hal - le - lu - jah, Hal-le - lu - jah, Hal-le - lu - jah, Hal-
11
A
-le - lu - jah, for the Lord God Om - ni - po-tent reign - eth, Hal-le-
-le - lu-jah, for the Lord God Om - ni - po-tent reign - eth, Hal-le-
-le - lu-jah, for the Lord God Om - ni - po-tent reign - eth, Hal-le-
-le - lu - jah, for the Lord God Om - ni - po-tent reign - eth, Hal-le-
A
15
-lu - jah, Hal-le - lu - jah, Hal-le - lu - jah, Hal-le - lu - jah,
-lu - jah, Hal-le - lu - jah, Hal-le - lu - jah, Hal-le - lu - jah, for the Lord
-lu - jah, Hal-le - lu - jah, Hal-le - lu - jah, Hal-le - lu - jah, for the Lord
-lu - jah, Hal-le - lu - jah, Hal-le - lu - jah, Hal-le - lu - jah, for the Lord

18
Hal-le - lu - jah, Hal-le - lu - jah, Hal-le -
God Om - ni - po-tent reign - eth, Hal-le - lu - jah, Hal-le - lu - jah, Hal-le -
God Om - ni - po-tent reign - eth, Hal-le - lu - jah, Hal-le - lu - jah, Hal-le -
God Om - ni - po-tent reign - eth, Hal-le - lu - jah, Hal-le - lu - jah, Hal-le -
21
B
-lu-jah, Hal-le-lu-jah, for the Lord God Om-ni - po - tent
-lu-jah, Hal-le-lu-jah, Hal-le-
-lu-jah, Hal-le-lu-jah, Hal-le-lu-jah, Hal-le-lu-jah, Hal-le-lu-jah, Hal-le -
-lu-jah, Hal-le-lu-jah,
B
24
reign - - - eth, Hal-le - lu - jah, Hal-le - lu - jah, Hal-le - lu -
- lu - jah, Hal - le - lu - jah, Hal-le - lu - jah, Hal-le - lu - jah, Hal - le - lu -
- - lu - jah, Hal-le - lu - jah, for the Lord
Hal-le - lu - jah, for the Lord

26
-jah, Hal-le-lu-jah, Hal-le-lu-jah, Hal-le-lu-jah,
-jah, Hal-le-lu-jah, Hal-le-lu-jah, Hal-le-
God Om-ni-po-tent reign-eth, Hal-le-lu-jah,
God Om-ni-po-tent reign-eth, Hal-le-
28
Hal-le-lu-jah, Hal-le-lu-jah, Hal-le-lu-jah, Hal-le-lu-jah,
-lu-jah, Hal-le-lu-jah, for the Lord
Hal-le-lu-jah, Hal-le-lu-jah, for the Lord
-lu-jah, Hal-le-lu-jah, Hal-le-lu-jah, Hal-le-
30
Hal-le-lu-jah, Hal-le-lu-jah, Hal-le-lu-jah, Hal-
God Om-ni-po-tent reign-eth, Hal-le-lu-jah,
God Om-ni-po-tent reign-eth, Hal-
-lu-jah, Hal-le-lu-jah, Hal-le-lu-jah, Hal-le-lu-jah, Hal-le-

32
C
- le - lu - jah! The King - dom of this world
Hal - le - lu - jah! The King - dom of this world
- le - - lu - jah! The King - dom of this world
- lu - jah, Hal - le - lu - jah! The King - dom of this world
C
36
is be - come the King - dom of our Lord and of His
is be - come the King - dom of our Lord and of His
is be - come the King - dom of our Lord and of His
is be - come the King - dom of our Lord and of His
40
D
Christ, and of His Christ;
Christ, and of His Christ;
Christ, and of His Christ; and He shall reign for
Christ, and of His Christ; and He shall reign for ev - er and ev - er, for ev - er and
tr
D

45
and He shall reign for ev - er and
ev - er and ev - - - er, and He shall reign for ev - er and
ev - er, and He shall reign, and He shall reign for ev-er, for
[tr]
48
and He shall reign for ev - er and ev - -
ev - - er, for ev-er and ev-er, for ev - er and
ev - - er, and He shall reign for ev-er and
ev-er and ev-er, for ev-er and ev-er, for ev - er, for ev-er and
[tr]
[tr]
51
E
-er, King of Kings,
ev - er, King of Kings,
ev - er, for ev - er and ev-er, Hal-le-lu-jah, Hal-le-
ev - er, for ev - er and ev-er, Hal-le-lu-jah, Hal-le-
E

54
and Lord of Lords, King of
and Lord of Lords,
-lu-jah, for ev-er and ev-er, Hal-le-lu-jah, Hal-le-lu-jah,
-lu-jah, for ev-er and ev-er, Hal-le-lu-jah, Hal-le-lu-jah,
58
Kings, and Lord of
for ev-er and ev-er, Hal-le-lu-jah, Hal-le-lu-jah,
for ev-er and ev-er, Hal-le-lu-jah, Hal-le-lu-jah,
for ev-er and ev-er, Hal-le-lu-jah, Hal-le-lu-jah,
61
Lords, King of
for ev-er and ev-er, Hal-le-lu-jah, Hal-le-lu-jah,
for ev-er and ev-er, Hal-le-lu-jah, Hal-le-lu-jah,
for ev-er and ev-er, Hal-le-lu-jah, Hal-le-lu-jah,

64
Kings, and Lord of
for ev - er and ev - er, Hal - le - lu - jah, Hal - le - lu - jah,
for ev - er and ev - er, Hal - le - lu - jah, Hal - le - lu - jah,
for ev - er and ev - er, Hal - le - lu - jah, Hal - le - lu - jah,
67
F
Lords, and Lord of Lords, and He shall
King of Kings, and Lord of Lords,
King of Kings, and Lord of Lords,
King of Kings, and Lord of Lords, and He shall
F
70
reign, and He shall reign for
and He shall reign, and He shall reign for
and He shall reign, and He shall reign, and He shall reign for
reign for ev - er and ev - er, and He shall

73
ev - er and ev - - er, for ev - er and ev - er,
ev - er and ev - - er, King of Kings, for ev - er and ev - er, and Lord of
ev - er and ev - - er, King of Kings, and Lord of
reign for ev - er and ev - er, King of Kings, for ev - er and ev - er, and Lord of
[tr]
77
Hal - le - lu - jah, Hal - le - lu - jah, and He shall reign for ev - er, for
Lords, Hal - le - lu - jah, Hal - le - lu - jah, and He shall reign for
Lords, and He shall reign for ev - er, for
Lords, Hal - le - lu - jah, Hal - le - lu - jah, and He shall reign for ev - er, for
80
G
ev - er and ev - - er, King of Kings, and Lord of
ev - er and ev - - er, King of Kings, and Lord of
ev - er and ev - - er, King of Kings, and Lord of
ev - er and ev - - er, King of Kings, and Lord of
tr
G

83
Lords, King of Kings, and Lord of Lords, and
Lords, King of Kings, and Lord of___ Lords, and
Lords, King of Kings, and Lord of___ Lords, and
Lords, King of Kings, and Lord of Lords, and He shall
86
He shall reign for ev - er and ev - - er, King of
He shall reign for ev - er and ev - - er, for ev - er and
He shall reign for ev - er and ev - - er, for ev - er and
reign for ev - er, for ev - er and ev - - er, for ev - er and
[tr]

OCCO 45 **Hallelujah Chorus** (SATB) HANDEL ed. BARTLETT

ISBN 0-19-341819-3
9 780193 418196